I'D LIKE TO BE THE WINDOW

For Wednesday most of all —P.S.

Copyright © 2022 by Philip C. Stead. All rights reserved. Published in the United States by Doubleday, an imprint of Random House Children's Books, a division of Penguin Random House LLC, New York. Doubleday and the colophon are registered trademarks of Penguin Random House LLC. Visit us on the Web! rhcbooks.com Educators and librarians, for a variety of teaching tools, visit us at RHTeachersLibrarians.com

Library of Congress Cataloging-in-Publication Data. Name: Stead, Philip Christian, author. | Title: I'd like to be the window for a wise old dog / words and pictures by Philip Stead. | Other titles: I would like to be the window for a wise old dog. | Description: First edition. | New York : Doubleday, [2022] | Audience: Ages 3–7. | Summary: "A wise old dog contemplates the limitless world of imagination through a window." —Provided by publisher. | Identifiers: LCCN 2020054483 (print) | LCCN 2020054484 (ebook) | ISBN 978-0-593-37508-2 (hardcover) | ISBN 978-0-593-37509-9 (library binding) | ISBN 978-0-593-37510-5 (ebook) | Subjects: CYAC: Imagination—Fiction. | Dogs—Fiction. | Classification: LCC PZ7.S808566 Ib 2022 (print) | LCC PZ7.S808566 (ebook) | DDC [E]—dc23

MANUFACTURED IN CHINA 10 9 8 7 6 5 4 3 2 1 First Edition

FOR A WISE OLD DOG

Words and pictures by
PHILIP STEAD

 DOUBLEDAY BOOKS FOR YOUNG READERS

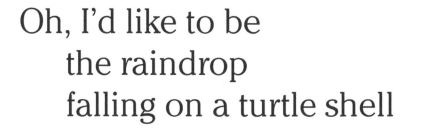

Oh, I'd like to be
    the raindrop
        falling on a turtle shell

I'd like to be
the puddle
for a big bullfrog

I'd like to be
   the welcoming umbrella
   of an elephant

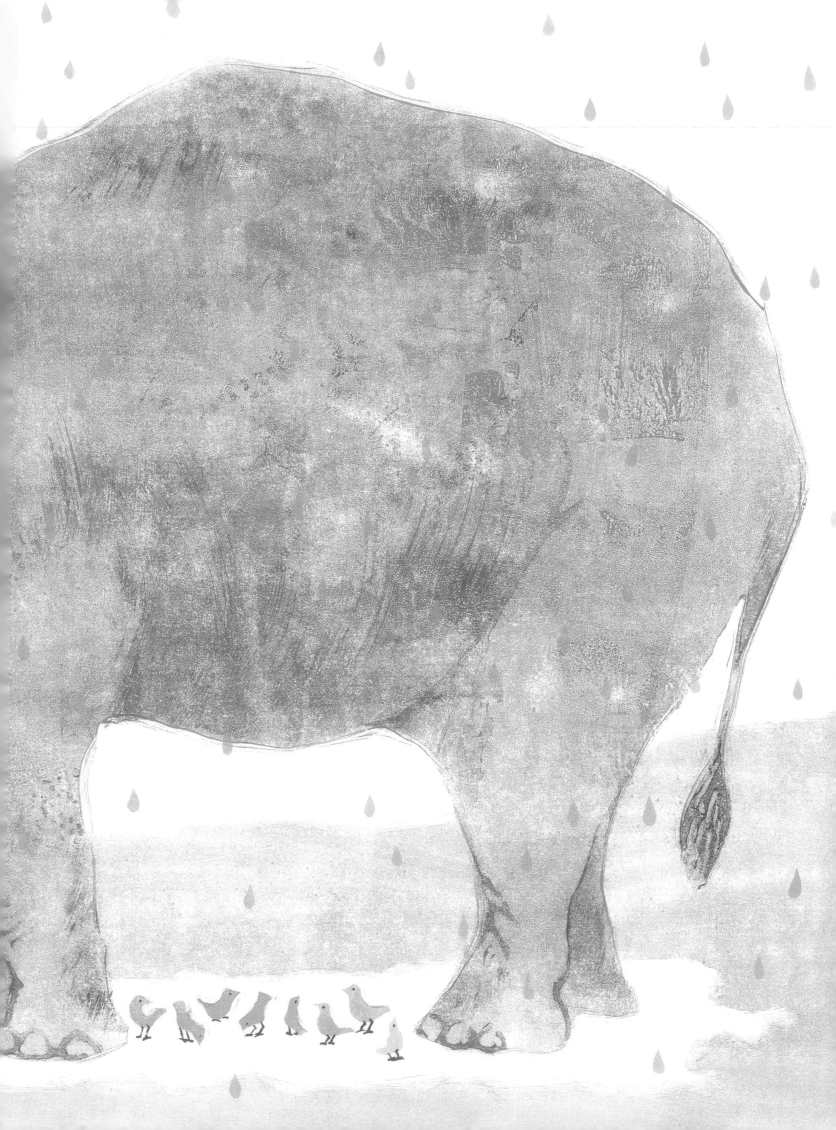

but most of all

and most of all

I'd like to be
    the window
        for a wise old dog

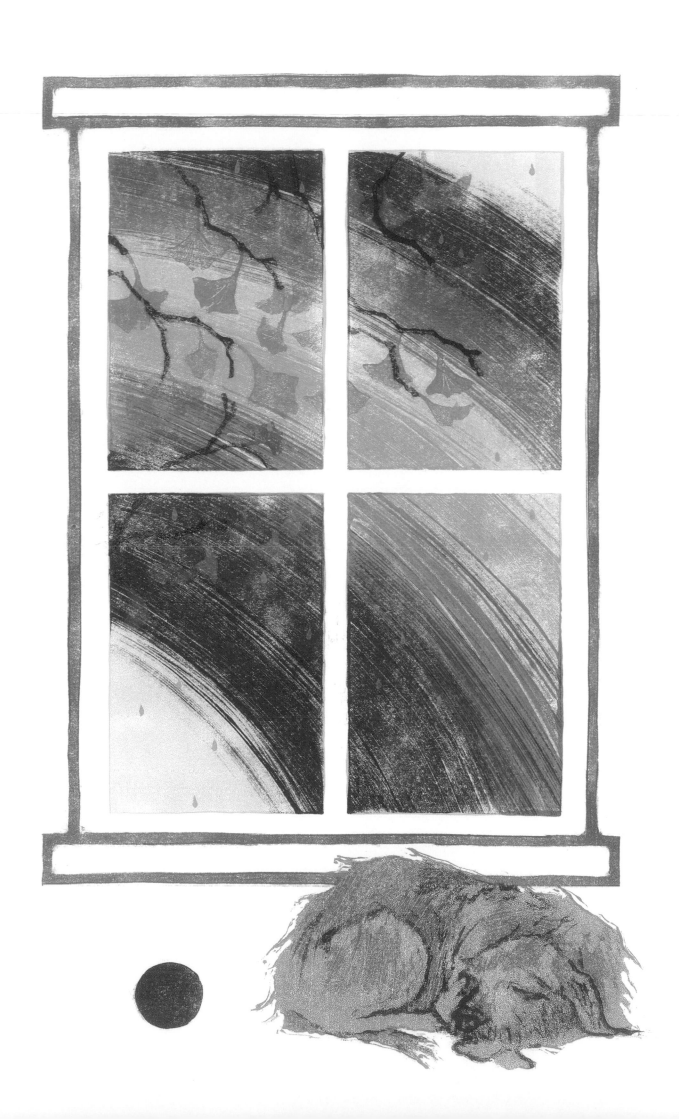

And I sometimes wonder . . .

Will I ever be
the dawdle of a penguin?

Will I ever be
the waddle of a snail?

Will I ever be
the tumble of a honeybee?

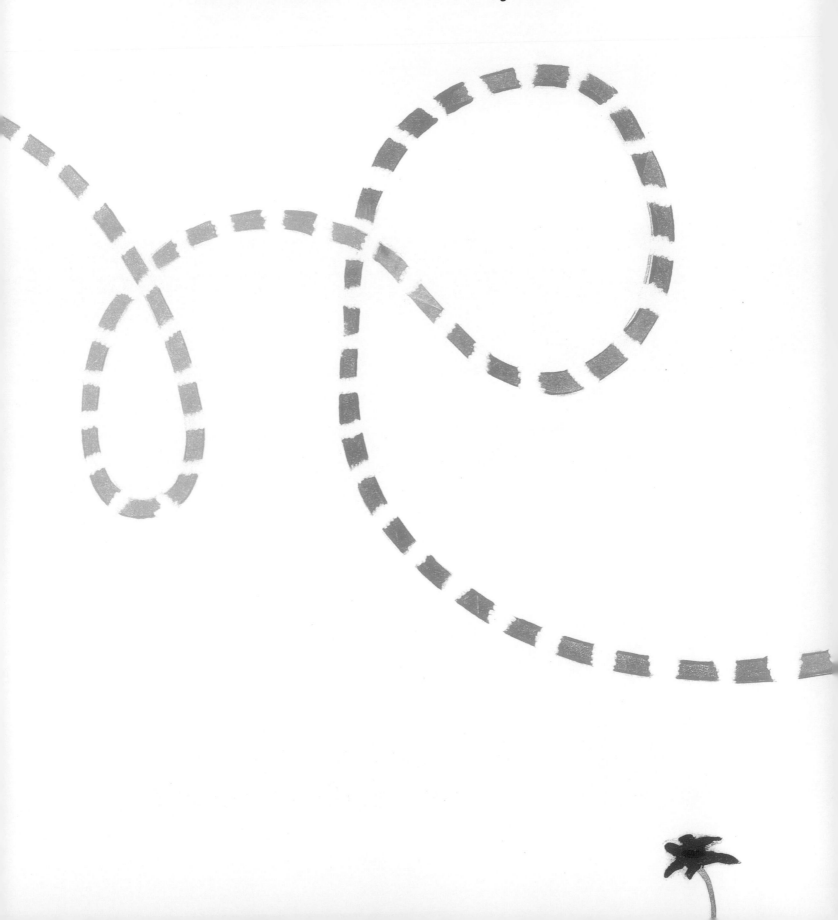

Will I ever be
the bumble . . .

. . . of a whale?

Oh, I don't know,
no, I don't know,

but I do know that . . .

I'd like to be
    the warm sun
        blanketing a buffalo

I'd like to be
   the hollow
     of an owl's oak tree

I'd like to be
the tall grass
standing with a mother deer
helping hide the little fawns

one   two   three

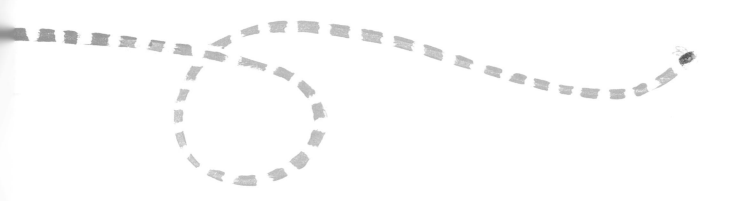

And I sometimes wonder . . .

Will I never be
    the feather of a walrus?

Will I never be
the weather of a wren?

Will I never be
the scurry of a hummingbird?

Will I never be
the hurry of a little mouse when . . .

the cat   sneaks slowly   by?

Oh, I don't know,
no, I don't know,

but I do know that . . .

I'd like to be
    the window
        for a wise old dog

who'll look through me
and wonder happily

about everything she's never been

and ever been

joyful and free.